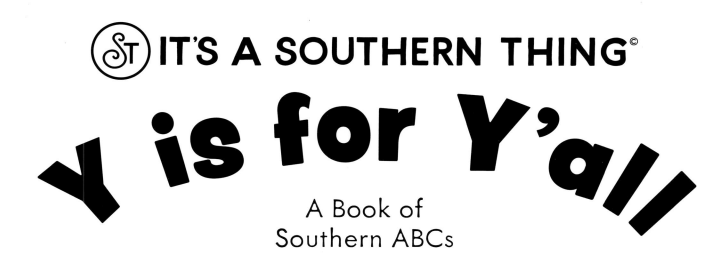

⑤T IT'S A SOUTHERN THING©

Y is for Y'all

A Book of Southern ABCs

Written by Kelly Kazek

Illustrated by Michelle Hazelwood Hyde

Visit us at **southernthing.com**

Printed in Canada
Second edition July 2020
ISBN: 978-1-57571-991-7 (hardback)

A is for azalea

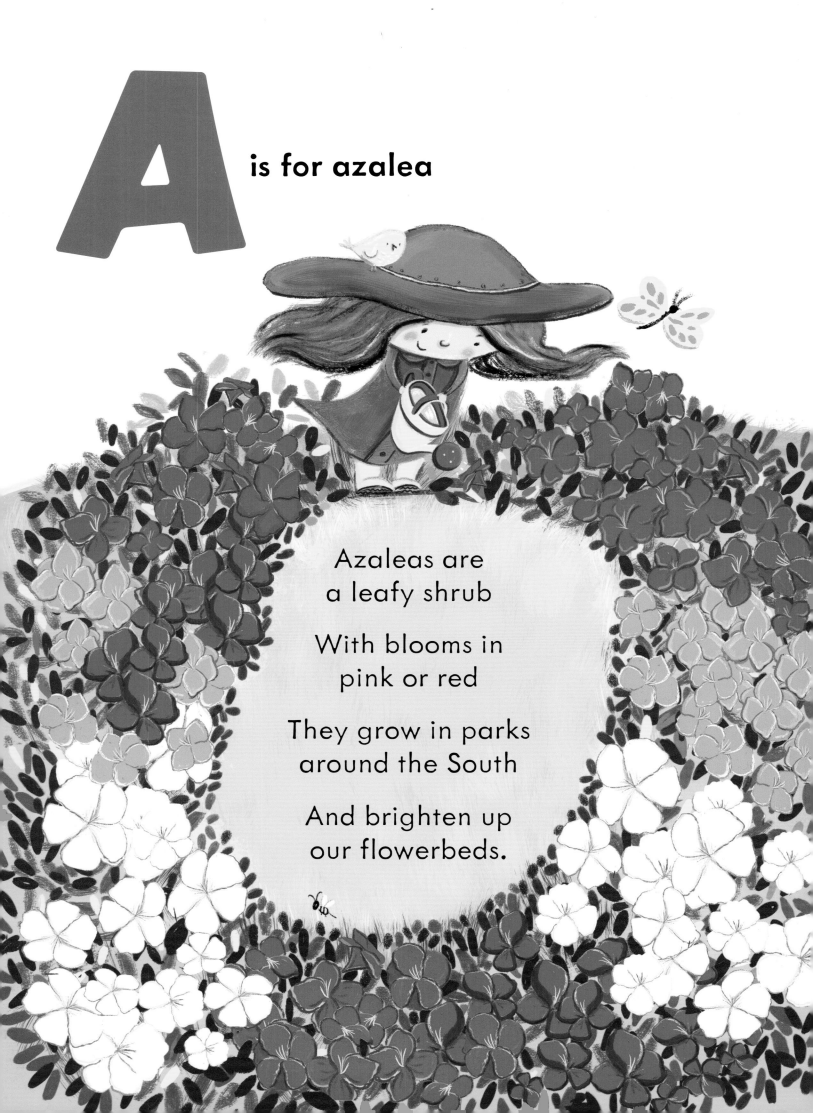

Azaleas are
a leafy shrub

With blooms in
pink or red

They grow in parks
around the South

And brighten up
our flowerbeds.

B

is for bless your heart

We spread this phrase around like hugs

"Bless her heart" and "his heart," too

It's something Southerners often say

When nothing else will do.

C

is for cornbread

This bread is made
from ground-up corn

That's stirred into
a batter

Then fried up like a
yummy cake

And served up on
a platter.

D is for deviled eggs

They make the
perfect portable treat

You can pop a
whole one in your mouth

You can find
as many as you want

At any potluck
in the South.

E is for étouffée

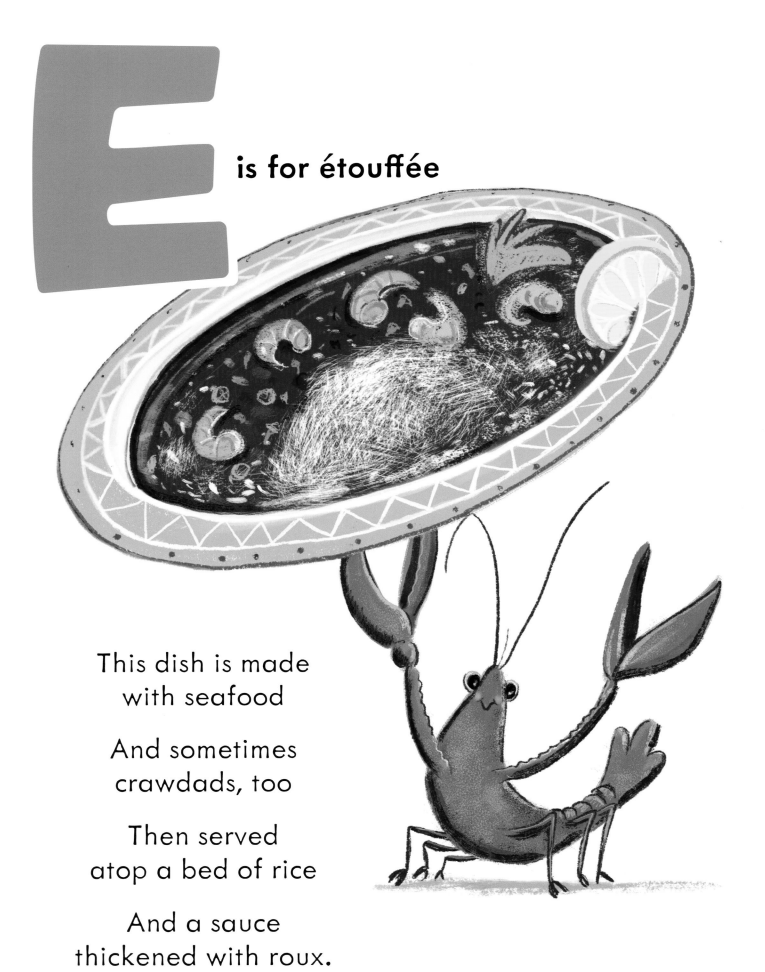

This dish is made
with seafood

And sometimes
crawdads, too

Then served
atop a bed of rice

And a sauce
thickened with roux.

F

is for fixin' to

If we make a plan to get something done

But we're not quite ready yet

We use the phrase "we're fixin' to"

Which means "in just a bit."

**is for
grits**

This Southern word is particular

About the way that it is writ

It can only be spelled with the "s"

There is no such thing as a "grit."

H

is for hissy fit

If you live in the South, you've heard it said

"Now don't have a hissy fit!"

But that wording is not entirely correct

Hissy fits aren't "had," they're "pitched."

is for insects

In summer, when you go outside

You never know what
things might greet you –

Mosquitoes, love bugs, gnats or flies,

Are all waiting there to eat you.

J is for jazz

Its peppy notes and
rhythmic tunes

Make your feet tap
to the beat

It fills the air in New Orleans

From Jackson Square
to Bourbon Street.

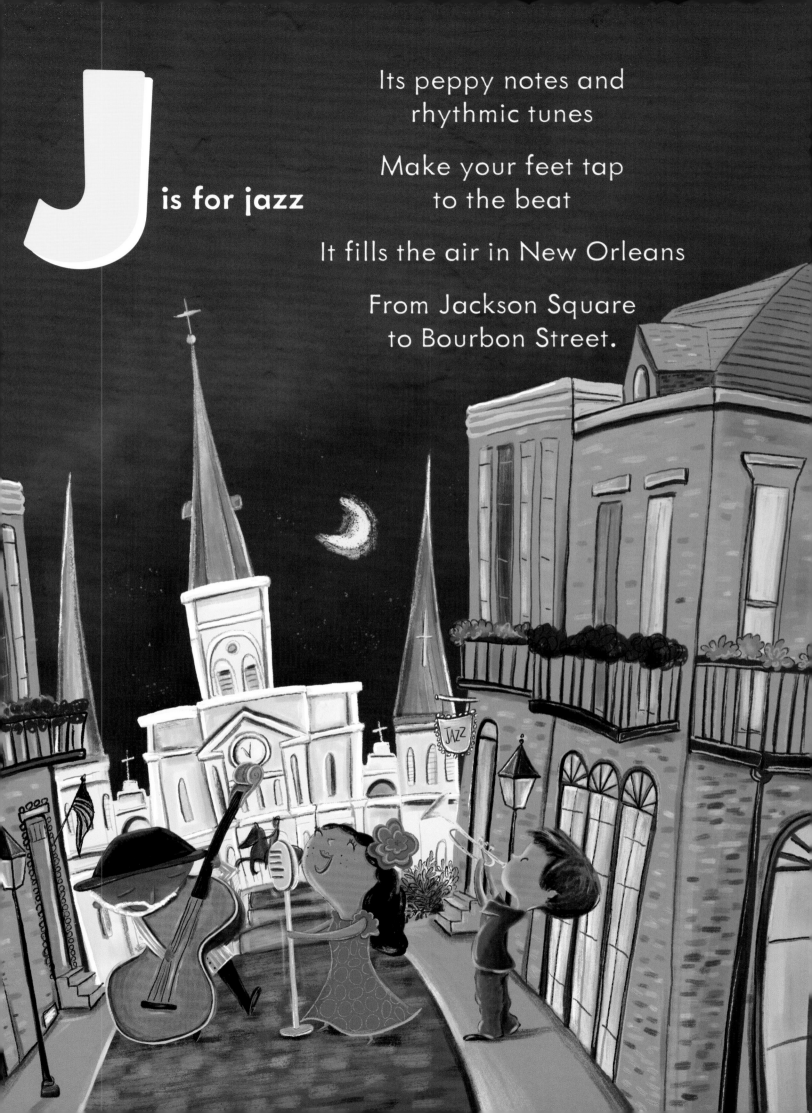

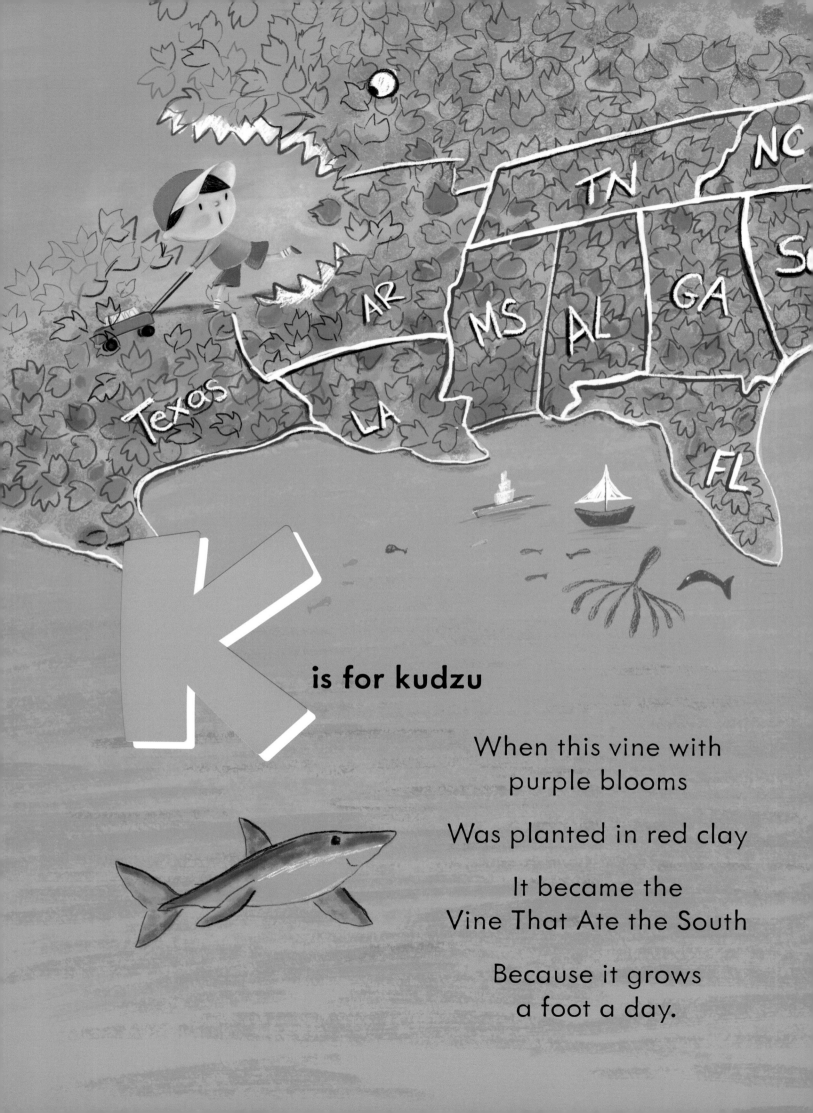

K is for kudzu

When this vine with
purple blooms

Was planted in red clay

It became the
Vine That Ate the South

Because it grows
a foot a day.

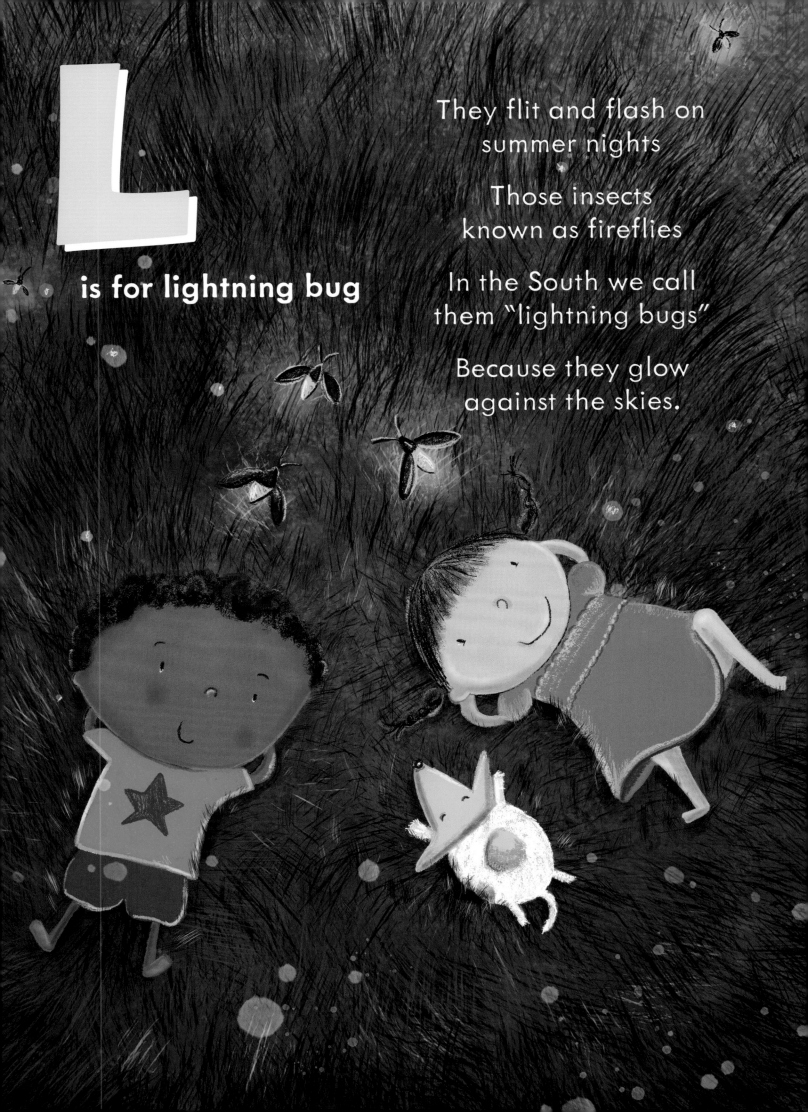

L

is for lightning bug

They flit and flash on summer nights

Those insects known as fireflies

In the South we call them "lightning bugs"

Because they glow against the skies.

M

is for magnolia

Its blooms are
soft and delicate

Its curling roots tenacious

Just like Southern women

Who are as tough as
they are gracious.

N

is for nanner puddin'

It's called "banana pudding"

If you speak properly and wooden

But those of us who are short on time

Just call it "nanner puddin'."

O is for okra

Boiling makes it squishy

Stewing makes it bland

Everyone knows it tastes the best

When fried up in a pan.

P is for peaches

Peaches are the perfect fruit

When picked fresh from the trees

But Grandma will bake them in a pie

If you ask her "pretty please."

Q is for quaint

The South is sometimes known as quaint

With its small towns and its farms

And friendly folks who just can't wait

To show you all its charms.

S

**is for
sweet tea**

Tea is fine when served up hot

In England they think that's nice

But when we drink it in the South

We like it served with sugar and ice.

T

is for tomato sandwich

Some people think tomatoes

Are perfect from the vine

But when you slice them on some bread

They really taste divine.

Mayonnaise

Bread

U is for umpteenth

Here's a made-up number you can use

To describe a large amount

If Mama says something "for the umpteenth time"

It means too many to count.

V

is for veranda

A "veranda" is a type of porch

Where we go to catch a breeze

And sit and pass the time of day

While drinking gallons of sweet tea.

W

is for watermelon

There are rules on how to eat

Large melons of this kind

You never eat them with a fork

You gnaw them to the rind.

is for xenial

It really means
"hospitable"

But if the word sounds
too complex

It's because it's the only
Southern word

We could find that
begins with "X."

Y is for y'all

We greet folks with, "Howdy, y'all,"

When meeting one-on-one

If there are groups of more than two

We say, "Are all y'all havin' fun?"

Z

is for zinnia

These cousins of the daisy

Are colorful and bright

They make a pretty spring bouquet

And bring smiles of delight.